One... two... three... four... five...

...six ...seven ...eight ...nine ...ten!

FOR LAUREN AND TOM – E.S.

EGMONT
We bring stories to life

First published in Great Britain 2011 by Egmont UK Limited
239 Kensington High Street, London W8 6SA

Text and illustrations copyright © Ellie Sandall 2011
The moral rights of the author/illustrator have been asserted

ISBN: 978 1 4052 5419 9 (hb)
ISBN: 978 1 4052 5457 1 (pb)

1 3 5 7 9 10 8 6 4 2

A CIP catalogue record for this title is available from the British Library

Printed and bound in Singapore

EGMONT

Daisy

plays Hide-and-Seek

Ellie Sandall

"Ready or not, here I come!"

shouted Jake. "You can't hide
from me, Daisy, you'll see!"

But Daisy is no ordinary cow.

Daisy is a strange, magical, COLOURFUL kind of cow.

And what's more,
she is ESPECIALLY GOOD
at playing hide-and-seek.

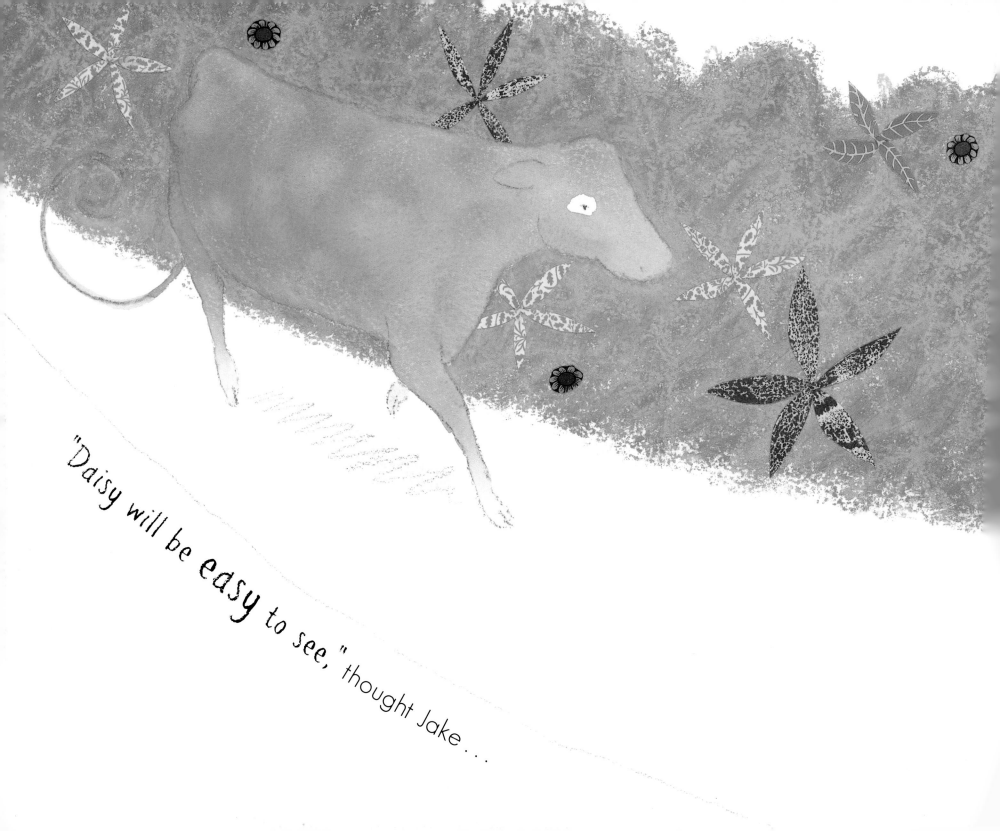

"Daisy will be **easy** to see," thought Jake . . .

and he set off to find her.

Jake looked in high places,

but he didn't see Daisy.

and low places,

He looked in **smelly** places,

muddy places,

and sparkling clean places,

but he didn't see Daisy.

Jake **skipped** through sunny places

and **crept** through spooky places.

and rustled through dry places,

but he didn't see Daisy.

He splashed through wet places,

Jake looked over,

and under,

in...

...and out.

Round and round, up, and down.

He looked **here,**

there,

and everywhere!

But he didn't see Daisy.

Jake could only think of one more place she could be.

He looked over the wooden gate,
and what did he see?

Cows!

Everywhere!

But...

...he STILL didn't see Daisy.

A single tear began to slide down his cheek.

He was about to give up.

But as he gazed sadly
at the grazing cows,

strangely,

magically,

COLOURFULLY
– he could see her!

"I told you I'd find you!" said Jake proudly.
He hugged her tight –

and Daisy turned
all of her **happiest** colours.

"You can't hide from me, Daisy,"
    said Jake. "You're just too easy to see!"

And strangely, magically, colourfully, they headed home.

One... two... three... four...